BEAR
needs a
HOME

Monica O'Neill
Illustrated by Brittany R. Jacobs

D1292620

Outskirts Press, Inc.
http://www.outskirtspress.com

Paperback ISBN: 978-1-9772-3942-6
Hardback ISBN: 978-1-9772-3948-8

Outskirts Press and the "OP" logo are trademarks belonging to Outskirts Press, Inc.

PRINTED IN THE UNITED STATES OF AMERICA

Based on a true story...

Once, there was a dog who
didn't know where his People were.
He felt scared and sad.
He didn't know what to do!

Suddenly, a familiar smell was in the air,

and for the first time since he got lost,
he knew he was not alone.

"Hello you,

would you like to come in out of the cold
and have something to eat?"

Relieved, he felt he could trust the Nice Lady.

"What is your name, fuzzy one?

Hmm... no name tag.

Let me take you back to the
animal shelter and check for your I.D. chip
to see if we can find your People."

"No chip either!"

"So sad," she said,
"all pets should have an I.D.
so people can help them if they get lost."

"We need to give you a bath!

So much dirt and stinky smell!"

"Now you look like a big ol' teddy bear!

I know, that is what I will call you, BEAR!"
And Bear it was from then on.

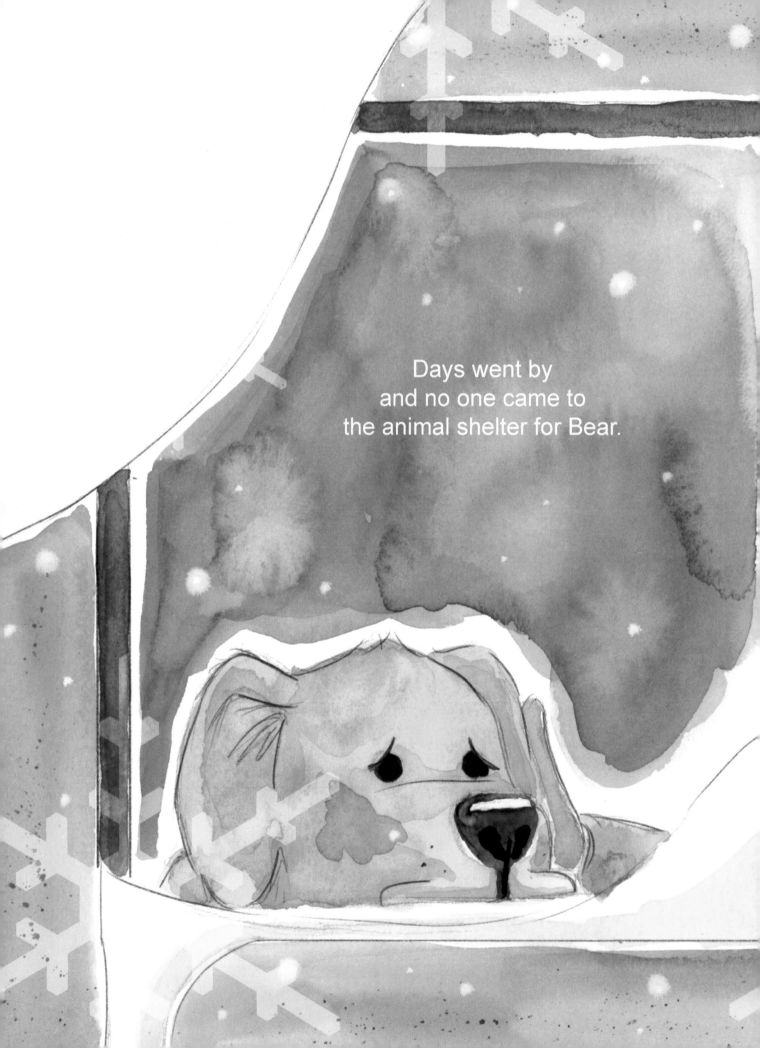

Days went by
and no one came to
the animal shelter for Bear.

"Sometimes people can't care for their pets anymore,

don't worry, Bear, we will take care of you!"

Bear was sad, but hopeful and glad he had food and a warm place to sleep.

But he really missed

running in parks,

playing with friends,

and being hugged

by his People.

Days went by while Bear waited,

and waited,

and waited.

The Nice Lady called every veterinarian,
pet rescue and fostering group,

"Bear needs a home!"

But they all said, "no, no, no."

Then one day she got a

yes!

"I will come and get him right now!"

"Are you sure?" said the Nice Lady,
"it's snowing very badly,
it looks like a blizzard!"

"I have a big red truck, we will be safe!"

As soon as Bear and the
Woman with the big red truck met,
they knew it was

friends forever!

She even brought treats for Bear!

"Good luck!"

And the Woman with the big
red truck helped Bear
into the back seat.

They headed out into the blizzard,
and the snow made driving
difficult and scary.

But, just as they got to their new
neighborhood the sun came out.

"Bear, do you want to stop and play?"
said the Woman with the big red truck.

As soon as the Woman opened the
red truck door, Bear burst out!

First, Bear met Elvis,
who loved chasing snow balls.

Then he met Cinnamon,
who was nervous and shook
for no reason but shyly said hello.

And Anna.

And Patxa,
she was a sheepdog
from Spain!

And Lucy,
with her pearls.

It was so much fun to run and play,
but the day was nearing an end.
His new friends headed home
with their People,
and Bear found the Woman with
the big red truck.

"Come on Bear,"
she said...

"its time to go
HOME."

Desi Fontaine Studios

Monica O'Neill is an author who lives in the
Washington, DC area. She wishes to thank
Golden Retriever Rescue Education and Training
(www.grreat.org) who brought Bear and her together,
a portion of the proceeds will be donated to
GRREAT. Please consider supporting your local
animal shelter and fostering organizations,
they really need our support.

Brittany R. Jacobs is an animal lover
and has rescued two dogs from Houston.
She is a children's book author/illustrator
and public librarian.
www.BrittanyRJacobs.com

CPSIA information can be obtained
at www.ICGtesting.com
Printed in the USA
BVHW021212130421
604826BV00011B/22